LTL

D0842726

4/00

✓

Mr. Wolf's Pancakes

With very special
thanks to Genevieve
and Ramona.

LITTLE TIGER PRESS
N16 W23390 Stoneridge Drive, Waukesha, WI 53188
First published in the United States 1999
Originally published in Great Britain 1999 by
Methuen Children's Books, London
Text and illustrations copyright © Jan Fearnley 1999
All rights reserved
CIP Data is available
ISBN I-888444-76-2
Printed in Hong Kong
First American edition
I 3 5 7 9 I0 8 6 4 2

Mr. Wolf's Pancakes

Jan Fearnley

Little Tiger Press

One day, Mr. Wolf was feeling hungry.
He decided to make some pancakes.
"Yum, yum," he said, licking his lips at the
thought of a big pile of fresh, delicious pancakes.

Mr. Wolf had never made pancakes before,
so he took his big recipe book down off the
shelf and looked inside.

But wolves can't read very well, and Mr. Wolf had trouble understanding it. So he went to get some help from his neighbors.

He called on Chicken Little who lived
next door.

"Can you please help me read this?" he asked.

"No!" said Chicken Little, slamming the
door in Mr. Wolf's face—BANG!

"Oh, dear," sighed Mr. Wolf. He sat down, slowly read the book, and worked out what he needed—all by himself.

Mr. Wolf looked in his cupboard for the ingredients,
but he couldn't find anything he needed.

"I'll go to the store," he decided, and he settled down
to write a list.

But wolves aren't very good at writing so Mr. Wolf
called on Wee Willy Winkle.

"You're very clever," said Mr. Wolf. "Can you help me write my shopping list, please?"

"No!" said Wee Willy Winkle. "Go away!" He slammed his door—BANG!

"There's no need to be like that," said Mr. Wolf quietly.

Mr. Wolf sat down and worked very hard at his writing until he had made his shopping list—all by himself.

Now he needed to count his money to make sure he had enough.

But wolves aren't very good at counting, so he went to the Gingerbread Man for some help.

"Can you help me count my money, please?"
he asked politely.

"No! I'm too busy to bother with you!"
said the Gingerbread Man, slamming his door—
BANG!

So poor Mr. Wolf had to sit down and count his money. It took him a long time, and he had to check it three times before it was right. But he did it—all by himself.

Mr. Wolf needed a basket to carry his groceries, so he called on Little Red Riding Hood.

"May I please borrow your basket?"
he asked very nicely.

"I'm not lending my basket to you!" said
Little Red Riding Hood. "Get out of here!"

So Mr. Wolf set off to the store
without a basket.

"I'll manage," he said.

Mr. Wolf went to the store.

He looked at his list, remembered what he
needed, counted out his money, and carried
the eggs, milk, and flour home—all by himself.

Now it was time to make the pancakes. But wolves aren't very good at cooking, so Mr. Wolf called on the Three Little Pigs.

"Can you please help me cook my pancakes? I'll share them with you," he said kindly.

"Forget about it!" chorused the pigs, slamming
their doors—BANG! BANG! BANG!

Mr. Wolf felt sad because nobody wanted
to help him.

Mr. Wolf went home and started to make the pancakes—all by himself.

Soon there was a huge pile of delicious pancakes on the table, all ready for eating.

Now, as Mr. Wolf had been making his pancakes, a lovely smell had drifted out of the kitchen.

All his neighbors could smell it, and it made them feel very hungry.

They wanted some pancakes, too.

They decided to try their luck.

So, they knocked on Mr. Wolf's door.

"Give us some of your pancakes!" said the rude bunch.

"Why should I give any to you?" said Mr. Wolf. "Not one of you would help me."

"We'll help you eat them," replied Mr. Wolf's neighbors nastily. "Anyway, we're not going away until you give us some!"

Mr. Wolf thought very hard for a moment.
There was only one decent thing to do.

"Oh, very well then," he sighed. "You had
better come in."

Mr. Wolf opened the door wide and—whoosh!—his greedy neighbors rudely pushed him aside and dashed down the hall.

Mr. Wolf shook his head, shrugged his shoulders, followed them into the kitchen, and when they were all in . . .

Mr. Wolf gobbled them up.

SNIPPITY! SNAPPITY!

That was the end of his unhelpful neighbors!

And then, with his bulging stomach still not full,
Mr. Wolf sat down to eat his pile of pancakes—and
he did it all by himself.

Well, there was nobody else around.